W9-BSL-755

TOUCHDOWN
TURMOIL

BY JAKE MADDOX

text by
Derek Tellier

STONE ARCH BOOKS
a capstone imprint

Jake Maddox JV Boys books are published by
Stone Arch Books
a Capstone imprint
1710 Roe Crest Drive
North Mankato, Minnesota 56003
www.mycapstone.com

Cataloging-in-Publication Data is available on the Library of Congress website.
ISBN: 978-1-4965-6331-6 (library binding)
ISBN: 978-1-4965-6333-0 (paperback)
ISBN: 978-1-4965-6335-4 (eBook PDF)

Summary: Ethan is a talented wide receiver for the Locomotives, but when he drops a surefire
touchdown pass, he begins to question himself.

Editor: Nate LeBoutillier
Designers: Tori Abraham and Charmaine Whitman

Photo Credits: Shutterstock: Brocreative, cover, back cover, 1, 4, 89, Danny E Hooks, chapter openers
(football), 92–93

Printed and bound in the United States of America.
PA021

TABLE OF CONTENTS

CHAPTER 1

HITCH-AND-GO

Ethan broke the huddle with his football team, the Humboldt Locomotives. He hustled out to the wide receiver spot near the sideline. He motioned to the official to see if he was on the line of scrimmage.

The ref nodded.

Ethan needed to be on the line to avoid an illegal formation penalty. Ethan never wanted to see a flag thrown. He especially wanted to avoid one on the coming play.

Coach Jennifer had called Ethan's number. The play, the hitch-and-go, was Ethan's favorite. The ball would be coming Ethan's way.

Ethan's buddy Gavin played quarterback for the Locomotives. Gavin went up under center and barked out some signals. "Locomotive one-nine. Locomotive one-nine."

The signals meant nothing. Coach Jennifer just wanted Gavin to say them to mix up the defense.

Gavin said, "Hut, hut!"

Ethan sprinted off the line of scrimmage. The defender ran back. He didn't want Ethan to get behind him. But after seven yards Ethan stopped, cut back, and looked for the ball.

Gavin reared his arm back and pump-faked as hard as he could. The defensive back expected a pass and closed in. That's when Ethan took off again. He busted up the field and got behind the defensive back.

Gavin tossed the ball over the defense, hitting Ethan in stride. Ethan raced into the end zone for a touchdown. The official raised his arms to signal the score.

Ethan's teammates slapped him on the shoulder pads. An offensive guard named Christian grabbed Ethan by the facemask and growled. He was, by far, the biggest of the eighth graders on the team. Growling was how Christian congratulated his teammates.

Gavin said, "Nice route, dude! Nice grab!"

The friends fist-bumped.

On the sideline, Coach Jennifer put her hand on Ethan's helmet. "We ran the hitch," she said. "Then we ran the hitch-and-go. That's how we set it up. Nice job, bud!"

Assistant Coach Bob gave Ethan a high-five. "Great pattern," he said.

Coach Jennifer addressed other players standing near. She said, "We aren't done. Those guys on the other sideline, they're the Shady Oak Raiders. You think they're done?"

Locomotives players shouted or shook their heads.

"That's right," said Coach Jennifer. "They're not done. We have to beat them one play at a time. One play at a time, Locomotives!"

The Locomotives lined up for the two-point conversion. The attempt failed, but they still led by six points.

The Shady Oak Raiders weren't done. They got the ball back and went to work with their bruising running attack.

On the first play, their shifty running back shimmied up the middle for twelve yards.

The next play, an option to the right, went for fourteen yards.

The next, an inside shuffle pass to the wingback, went for seventeen yards.

The Locomotives defense was on their heels. Then the Raiders tossed the ball to the left, which was a mistake.

Christian, the Locomotives growly offensive guard, also played on the defensive line. The left was his side. Christian crashed through the blockers. He stuck the tailback for a six-yard loss.

Christian stood up and growled. He pounded on his chest. He wanted to fire up the defense.

The Raiders kept marching. They ran an option to the left.

Christian came in. Though he walloped the quarterback, the QB tossed the ball to the shifty running back. The back scrambled around the end for a first down.

On the next play, the quarterback faked left and bootlegged to the right. The Locomotives defense expected him to keep it, but as they came charging in, he threw it. His pass hit the Raiders tight end on an out route.

The Locomotives defense was out of position.

The Raiders tight end turned the ball up the field and went in for a score. After the Raiders scored on the two-point conversion, the Locomotives trailed by two. It was late in the fourth quarter.

On the sideline, Ethan and Gavin fist-bumped. Gavin said, "Let's get 'em back."

Ethan said, "One play at a time."

The Raiders kicked off and pinned the ball deep. The Locomotives offense huddled, called a pass play, and broke.

Ethan hustled out to his wideout position. He made sure he was on the line.

Gavin called out, "Locomotive two-seven!" The signal again was only meant to try to fool the defense. "Locomotive two-seven! Hut, hut!"

Gavin dropped back to pass. He didn't see anyone open, so he ran through some space in the middle for a short gain.

The next few plays, Gavin dumped off a couple short passes to Kenny and Jason, the other receivers on the squad. Then he hit Ethan on a crossing route to move the chains.

The Locomotives then gained some yards on the ground. Time was winding down.

Coach Jennifer sent in a play for Ethan. It was another hitch pattern.

When Gavin took the snap and dropped back, Ethan charged off the line like he was going deep. The corner thought Ethan was actually going deep and stayed back. He did not want to get burned like on Ethan's last touchdown.

But Ethan fooled him. Ethan stopped, cut back, and looked for the ball.

Gavin's pass hit Ethan right in the numbers. The defender recovered and made the tackle, but Ethan had enough for a first down.

The Locomotives mixed in some runs. Gavin hit Kenny and Jason on some out patterns. The ball was on the Raiders 18-yard line.

The Locomotives called a timeout with thirty seconds remaining.

Coach Jennifer ran out onto the field. To her huddled team, she said, "We got 'em fooled. They can't cover us. We're going back to the hitch-and-go."

The players took their positions after the timeout. Ethan made sure he was on the line of scrimmage.

Gavin barked, "Locomotive eighteen. Locomotive eighteen. Hut, hut!"

Ethan stampeded down the field. He stopped, cut back, and looked for the ball.

When Gavin pump-faked, the defensive back just froze. He couldn't tell if the offense was going short or going long. Ethan dashed up the field and got behind the frozen defender.

Gavin slung the ball in a tight spiral. It arched through the air into Ethan's hands. Ethan could feel its leather under the sticky fingers of his receiver gloves. He looked up field and . . .

He no longer felt the ball.

Ethan stopped running and turned around. The ball was lying on the ground.

He had dropped it.

Ethan couldn't believe it. He had run the pattern a million times. He had caught the ball a million times.

He tried to figure out what had happened. What was it? He must have taken his eyes off the ball as he looked upfield.

The Locomotives tried another pass play, but the Raiders sacked Gavin and time ran out. Ethan's dropped pass had cost his team the game.

CHAPTER 2

EMERGING VICTORIOUS

Ethan came out of the bathroom after taking a shower. Dad was sitting on the couch, shaking his head, and fiddling around with his phone. He belonged to some college football chat groups. He liked to argue with people about matchups, strategy, rankings, key players, injuries—you name it.

Dad showed Ethan a comment QB3000 had left. It said, *Auburn beats 'Bama on Saturday by ten!*

Dad laughed. He said, "Auburn can't stop Alabama's offense. They can't stop Alabama's defense. They can't stop Alabama's special teams. QB3000 ought to come back to the present."

Ethan plopped down on the couch. He didn't say anything.

Dad lowered his phone and said, "Should we get some superglue to put on your gloves? That's what the Patriots do."

"No they don't," said Ethan.

"Yeah they do," Dad said. "They deflate balls and glue up their gloves."

"Says who?" said Ethan.

"QB3000," said Dad.

"I don't need any glue on my gloves," said Ethan.

"I know you don't need any glue on your gloves," Dad said. "Want to have a pizza?"

"No," Ethan said.

"I don't either," Dad said. "Pizza is overrated. Let's go do some one-handers."

They turned on the yard lights and grabbed a ball out of the garage. Ethan jogged a fly pattern. Dad lofted a floater Ethan caught with one hand.

Ethan tossed the ball back and ran an out route. This time, Dad fired it. Again, Ethan caught the ball with one hand.

Dad said, "Use one hand in games. Coach Jennifer will love it."

"I'd get benched," Ethan said.

"Probably," Dad said. "Run a slant."

Ethan lined up.

Dad nodded as a signal to start the play. Ethan took one step and then cut to the inside. He slanted up the would-be field, which, of course, was the yard. Dad delivered a bullet, and Ethan brought it in with one hand.

"Awesome," Dad said. "These one-handers make you watch the ball more."

Ethan tossed the ball to Dad, who caught it and fired it right back. Ethan tried to one-hand it, and he almost made a clean catch. He bobbled it enough to snap it out of the air and pull it into his chest. He acted like he was getting two feet in bounds along the sideline and, for effect, fell down.

Dad ran up to make the "complete" signal. He said, "First down!"

While Ethan was still lying on the ground, Dad said, "Get up and run a hitch-and-go."

Ethan stayed on the ground.

Dad said, "Well, I guess you can get back on the horse tomorrow."

***

In bed that night, Ethan rolled around. He couldn't sleep. The dropped hitch-and-go in the game haunted him. He just couldn't believe it.

The hitch-and-go was his favorite play, his bread and butter. He balled up wads of the sheet in his fists. He squeezed as hard as he could until his hands hurt.

At school the next day, Ethan saw Christian, the growly lineman, in the hall.

Christian said, "You sleep last night?"

Ethan said, "Not really."

"Me neither," said Christian. "I was too jacked up. How do you feel today?"

"Not super great," Ethan said.

"Yeah," said Christian. "You got to catch those."

Ethan didn't know if Christian was kidding or not. Christian wore a frown—but that was sort of how he always looked. So Ethan just said, "I know."

Christian growled. He slapped Ethan on the shoulder and walked off.

Ethan didn't know Christian very well. He didn't know what to make of Christian's remark. What if Christian was more upset than Ethan realized? Ethan's stomach dropped, and suddenly he felt like hitting the nurse's office.

Ethan entered a classroom and sat down next to Gavin, whose eyelids looked droopy. Maybe Gavin hadn't slept much either. Ethan figured his dropped pass must have ruined the night for his QB. It probably ruined the night for the entire team.

The teacher assigned a bunch of math problems. Ethan was yawning and having trouble paying attention. He asked Gavin if he knew the answer to one of the problems.

Gavin said no even though Ethan could see that Gavin had finished the problem. Ethan wondered if this had something to do with the dropped pass.

The teacher went over the answers. Ethan got a few more wrong than he usually did, but he didn't really care. He was mad because other people were mad.

He had never screwed up a play to lose a game. In fact, on many occasions, he had made the game-winning plays. A losing play? The feeling was new.

Ethan hated it. It stunk. It stunk worse than his socks. Worse than his cleats. Worse than his gear after a practice in August. It was ripe.

Ethan thought he might have to throw up, so he got a hall pass. Once he got to the restroom, he decided that he didn't have to. He did want to sit in private, though. He went into the stall and shut the door. He leaned up against one of the walls and squirmed.

He replayed the dropped pass in his head. He remembered rushing off the line of scrimmage, stopping, cutting back, and looking for the ball. He remembered Gavin's pump-fake. He remembered busting upfield, past the defensive back.

This time, he watched the ball closely and imagined bringing it in with one hand. No problem. *Touchdown!* But this was just his imagination.

In the real world, he had left his classroom and was leaning with his head against a wall in the bathroom. Ethan didn't know what he was doing.

He was so upset that he wandered the halls for a few minutes. He stopped at a drinking fountain and took a long drink, swallowing the cold water.

He told himself that he would have to do better. He would get tougher mentally. He would sharpen his concentration and not take any plays for granted. He would never let his team down.

The hitch pattern was his.

He owned it.

The hitch-and-go pattern was his.

He owned it.

He owned every ball thrown in the air.

He was Ethan, and he would emerge victorious.

DISAPPOINTMENT
DISAPPEARS

That day at practice, Coach Jennifer and Assistant Coach Bob gathered their guys at the 50-yard line.

Coach Jennifer said, "Locomotives, I didn't sleep well last night."

Assistant Coach Bob said, "I didn't either."

Christian growled in Ethan's ear. Ethan shook his head and rolled his eyes.

Coach Jennifer continued. "We did a lot of things right, but we came up short. It was a tough one."

Assistant Coach Bob said, "Games like those will eat you to pieces."

The game had already eaten Ethan to pieces. Ethan wondered how long this speech was going to last.

"What you have to do," Assistant Coach Bob said, "is put it behind you. We're the Humboldt Locomotives."

"It's on all of us," said Coach Jennifer. "It's not on the defense. It's not on Ethan. It's on all of us."

Ethan felt the loss actually *was* his fault. He had vowed to do better. He had vowed to emerge victorious. Coach Jennifer saying the loss was not Ethan's fault just made him feel bad again.

"Everyone get in here," Coach Jennifer said.

The guys gathered in as tightly as they could. In unison, they started bobbing their shoulders back and forth. They were going to get fired up. Coach Jennifer and Assistant Coach Bob clapped their hands rhythmically. The players bobbed their shoulders.

Coach Jennifer clapped twice and said, "Energy!"

The guys clapped twice. They said, "Energy!"

The players bobbed back and forth.

Assistant Coach Bob clapped his hands twice. He said, "Energy!"

The guys clapped twice. They said, "Energy!"

Coach Jennifer clapped twice. She said, "Humboldt!"

The guys clapped twice. They said, "Humboldt!"

Both coaches said, "One, two, three!"

All the players yelled, "*HUMBOLDT*!" And they ran as fast as they could to their individual stations.

The wideouts began their drills on the blocking dummies. Ethan got himself ready. He lined up five yards away from a dummy.

Assistant Coach Bob blew his whistle.

Ethan exploded forward. He put his shoulder into the blocking dummy and pumped his legs. He drove it backward for ten yards.

The pushing felt great and let him take out his frustrations. He wanted to shove that dummy from one end of the field to the other.

"Atta boy, Ethan," said Assistant Coach Bob. "Way to drive it with your legs."

"I'll growl at it next time," Ethan said.

"We already have one growler," Assistant Coach Bob said. "I don't know if I can handle any more."

Ethan got in line to nail the dummy again. He put a good number of hard hits on it. He felt some disappointment disappear.

Pass-catching drills came next. The guys played some catch and lined up for the one-on-one drill: one receiver against one defensive back. The quarterback would call out a pattern. The receiver and the defender could both hear it.

The trick was to make the play even when the defense knew what was coming.

Ethan's first time up, Gavin called a flag pattern. Ethan would need to run six yards down the field, slant inside for three yards, and then break to the outside and run toward the pylon. In the one-on-one drill, this was a tough one to complete.

All the defender had to do was hang back and not let the receiver get behind him.

Gavin dropped back.

Ethan sprinted down the field. He made his cuts and broke toward the pylon.

Gavin threw a tight spiral deep down the field. The defender moved in to make a play on the ball, but Ethan kept his body between the ball and the defensive back and made the catch.

His opponent tackled him, but Ethan held on. Catching the pass and taking the hit felt great. Ethan was focused and regaining his swagger.

Ethan's next time, Gavin called the hitch-and-go. Ethan was glad—he would have to get back on the horse sooner or later.

Gavin called out signals and dropped back. Ethan fired off the line of scrimmage. He stopped and cut back. The defender knew what was coming, but Gavin pump-faked anyway. Ethan broke up the field. Again, the defensive back was right on him.

Gavin fired.

The defender made a play but bumped Ethan hard before the ball arrived. It was pass interference, but Ethan got back on course, stuck out one hand, and brought in the ball.

Coach Jennifer, who was working with the lineman nearby, saw the play. She trotted over to help Ethan up and give him a high-five. "Nice job," she said. "Nice concentration."

Ethan felt like he would never drop a pass again.

***

At home, Dad was cooking a salmon fillet on the stove. The kitchen smelled like fish, an aroma Ethan despised. Dad took his hand and wafted some fish-smoke into his nostrils. He breathed in deeply through his nose and savored the smell.

Ethan ignored his dad's behavior. He asked. "Can we get a blocking dummy?"

"A blocking dummy?" Dad said. "Why?"

"If you screw up the game," Ethan said, "it's fun to shove them around."

"I bet so," said Dad. "You think I could shove this blocking dummy around? You know, give it the business when I came home from work?"

"Probably."

"I'll think about it, then," said Dad. "Run any hitch-and-goes at practice?"

"We did in the one-on-one." Ethan plugged his nose. He waived fish smell out of his face.

"You get back on your horse?" asked Dad.

"For sure," said Ethan. His voice was stuffy from plugging his nose.

"Sounds like things are headed in the right direction," said Dad. "You know, I've been thinking. You ought to try positive visualization. It's another thing that could help."

Ethan didn't respond.

Dad went on. "Positive visualization is pretty simple," he said. "You just have to learn how to concentrate hard. Then you focus in on an imaginary scene where you see yourself succeeding. If you picture yourself succeeding, you will."

Ethan still didn't respond. He didn't want to hear about positive visualization.

"The trick is," said Dad, "to do it again and again until it feels normal. And you have to concentrate hard. You have to focus."

Ethan waved his hand in front of his face. He said, "Dad, I'm good."

LOSING THE BATTLE

For the next game, the Humboldt Locomotives visited the Redville Red Hawks, one of the tougher teams in the conference. After losing to Shady Oak, the Locomotives needed a win.

The Locomotives were excited. The players, Coach Jennifer, Assistant Coach Bob—everyone.

On the sideline, right before kickoff, Coach Jennifer rounded up the team. She said, "I want to know who's fired up!"

The players yelled, "We're fired up!"

Assistant Coach Bob said, "Who's fired up?"

The players yelled, "We're fired up!"

Both coaches said, "One, two, three . . . "

And the players yelled, "HUMBOLDT!"

The Locomotives kick receiving team took the field. The Red Hawks kicker booted a line-drive kick to an up-back. The back stumbled ahead a few yards. The Locomotives took possession of the football at their own 42-yard line.

Coach Jennifer called Ethan's number. The play? A hitch. The plan was to set up the hitch-and-go.

Ethan motioned to the official to make sure he was on the line of scrimmage. The official said he was.

Gavin barked some fake signals. "Locomotives eight-nine. Locomotives eight-nine. Hut, hut!"

The defensive back bumped Ethan as he came off the line. Since the contact occurred within five yards of scrimmage, no pass interference was called. Ethan broke to the outside to run around the defender.

The defender stuck with him. Then Ethan cut back out of his route.

Gavin gunned the ball right into Ethan's stomach. Complete. The defensive back and safety then drove Ethan into the ground.

Christian gave Ethan a growl and slapped him on the back as the guys ran back to the huddle.

In the huddle, Gavin grabbed Ethan. Gavin said, "If they want to play that tight, let 'em. The hitch-and-go will be wide open."

Ethan agreed and could not wait to scorch them on the deep route. The guys thumped each other on the shoulder pads and got back to work.

The Locomotives mixed in some runs and short passes. Coach Jennifer had Ethan running slants and four-yard out-routes. The Red Hawks cornerbacks kept playing tight coverage. Coach Jennifer figured it was time to go deep and called the hitch-and-go.

Ethan checked with the official to make sure he was on the line. The official gave him a thumbs-up.

Gavin tried to hide the big smile on his face and got under center with his mouth guard half in and half out. Then he got serious and put his mouth guard in. "Humboldt," he said. "Humboldt. Hut, hut!"

The Red Hawks bumped Ethan as he came off the line. Ethan fought through all the shoving. He stopped and cut his route back. Gavin pump-faked. The defenders bit, and Ethan broke up the field. He was wide open.

Gavin stuck the ball behind his ear and spiraled a pass over the defense.

Ethan watched the ball. It landed perfectly in his hands. He felt its leather under his sticky receiver gloves, and then . . .

It was gone. He had dropped it once again. The pass was incomplete.

Ethan stared at the ball as it rolled to a halt near a yard marker. He couldn't believe it.

The ball had been right in his hands. He would have easily scored a touchdown.

Things in the huddle got a little awkward.

No one growled or slapped Ethan on the shoulder pads. No one told him to do better next time. No one got in his face. The other players seemed as shocked as Ethan was.

Coach Jennifer called a running play, a sweep. Luckily for Ethan, the ball carrier was going to come his way. Ethan felt like delivering a bone-crushing block, like what he had done with the blocking dummy at practice.

The snap. The toss.

Ethan drove the corner off the line about seven yards and could see the running back sprinting behind him and going to the outside.

Ethan broke off his block and picked up a safety who was zooming in. Ethan's blocks sprung the ball carrier for a Locomotives touchdown.

The blocks felt great, but Ethan wondered how he could have dropped that hitch-and-go. He had vowed to snag everything in the air. He had failed.

Christian growled at Ethan and smacked him excitedly in the helmet. "Nice block, dude!" he said.

Gavin gave Ethan a fist-bump. "Way to recover," he said.

Ethan knew what Gavin meant, but still. He felt ashamed that he even needed to recover.

Once Ethan got to the sideline, Coach Jennifer ran up. She popped him on the shoulder pads. "Fantastic block," she said. "Fantastic block!"

Ethan appreciated the compliment, but he couldn't stop thinking about dropping the ball.

Assistant Coach Bob could tell Ethan was upset. He put his arm around Ethan. "Something like this happened to me once," he said. "We'll talk at practice."

***

At home after the game, Ethan and Dad sat on the couch and poked at their devices. Dad argued with QB3000. Ethan tried his best to completely zone out on a video game.

Dad could tell Ethan was not happy about dropping another pass. "I don't want to see any moping," Dad said. "You won the game."

"The pass was right in my hands," said Ethan.

"Who cares?" said Dad. "You made the block on the next play."

"Coach never would have called that play if I had caught the ball," said Ethan.

Dad put his phone in his pocket. "You played good team ball," said Dad. "Everyone stepped up. You had each other's backs."

"I don't want anyone to have my back," said Ethan. "I should have caught the pass."

"You can't do everything," said Dad. "That's why you have a team. You need to work together."

"I can't get it out of my head," said Ethan.

In Ethan's video game, the receiver dropped a long bomb that could have gone for a touchdown. Ethan couldn't believe it. He caught himself nearly throwing the controller down.

"Want me to teach you the art of positive visualization?" asked Dad.

"No," said Ethan. "I don't."

"Well," said Dad, "if you don't stop moping, I'm going to."

Ethan smiled, but deep down inside, he was still kicking himself.

CHAPTER 5

YIPS AND DROPS

In class the next day, Ethan and Gavin were sitting next to each other. As they worked on their assignments, Ethan told Gavin, "I've got to get that hitch-and-go."

"Dude," said Gavin, "you've gotten that play a million times."

"I know," said Ethan. "But I can't get the drops out of my head."

"Maybe Christian could growl them out or something," said Gavin.

"My dad wants to teach me positive visualization," said Ethan.

"What's that?" asked Gavin.

"I don't know exactly," said Ethan. "It's probably something weird."

The guys went back to their assignments.

***

After practice, Ethan stayed late. He and Assistant Coach Bob went jogging around the athletic grounds. They talked about the aggressive play of the Red Hawks defensive backs.

Finally, Assistant Coach Bob said, "You want to hear a stupid story?"

"How stupid is it?" asked Ethan.

"It's pretty stupid," said Assistant Coach Bob.

"Fire away," said Ethan.

"When I was your age," said Assistant Coach Bob, "I was like you, but with basketball. I spent a lot of time thinking about the game, practicing, and playing."

Ethan had no idea Assistant Coach Bob had ever played basketball. Ethan only knew him from football. But as long as the story was sports-related, Ethan would listen.

Assistant Coach Bob said, "I was the starting point guard on the traveling basketball team. Offensively, I could shoot, drive, and dish. Defensively, I had a knack for moving my feet and getting into position to take charges. By doing so, I caused turnovers and got inside opponents' heads."

Ethan said, "I'm wondering exactly what this story has to do with me and my situation."

Assistant Coach Bob smiled. "Hear me out," he said. "So I averaged about fourteen points and eight assists per game. I forced a few turnovers every game by taking charges. Suddenly, in the middle of the season, my stats skyrocketed. I started scoring twenty points and dishing out twelve assists per game." Assistant Coach Bob paused and shook his head. "It was at that point I got the yips."

"The yips?" said Ethan.

"The yips are like the drops," said Assistant Coach Bob. "During one of my games, a teammate had scrapped for a rebound. The teammate saw me open for a fifteen-foot jump shot and dished me the ball. I took the shot, but I bricked it. The shot felt normal, but I absolutely bricked it."

Ethan smiled. He appreciated the honesty. He said, "So did the missed shot mess you up?"

"Big time," said Assistant Coach Bob. "Suddenly I couldn't make anything. The next time I got open for a shot, I squared up and took it. Like before, everything felt normal, but the shot went clanging off the rim. Later in the game, I drew a foul and went to the line. I was an eighty-five-percent free throw shooter, but I missed both free throws. The second one was an airball. Later, I missed a wide open lay-up."

"Wow," said Ethan.

Assistant Coach Bob said, "If the yips want you, there's nothing you can do to stop them."

"That doesn't make me feel too great," said Ethan.

"It got worse before it got better," said Bob. "Defenses stopped guarding me, so no passes were open. My numbers went way down. I was scoring only a few baskets per game." He shook his head. "I had the yips, bad."

"Tell me you got rid of them," Ethan said.

"It was tricky," said Bob. "You have to pick up other aspects of your game. The yips controlled my offensive game but not my defensive game. So I shot less and fought back on defense. My progress seemed to be backward. Going back to the basics was hard, but it was what I had to do. It actually made me mad."

"That's sort of how I feel," said Ethan.

"It was easy to take out that frustration by playing tighter defense," said Assistant Coach Bob. "I came away with a few more steals here and there. Causing turnovers on defense got me fired up. I worked on my rebounding. I tried to be a good teammate."

"Did that work?" asked Ethan.

"Slowly," said Assistant Coach Bob, "the yips unwound. In one game I stole a couple passes and went in for uncontested lay-ups. I felt some confidence return. Later in that game, I got fouled and went to the line. I sank both free throws. Then the next time down the court, I sank a fifteen-foot jump shot."

"Is that when you lost the yips?" asked Ethan.

"Yep," said Assistant Coach Bob. "I knew at that point that I was back. Not that I made every shot. But I could wheel and deal again. I could play more freely. I didn't have anything in the back of my mind telling me not to."

"What should I do to get over the drops?" Ethan asked. "Block people?"

"That's what I'd do," said Assistant Coach Bob. "It's another aspect of your game. You could dominate there, get your head straight."

"Believe me," said Ethan. "I feel like putting some blocks on people."

"Yeah," said Bob. "The yips make you mad."

"They're monsters," said Ethan.

"They kind of are," said Assistant Coach Bob. "If you can pick up your blocking game, you should be fine. If not . . . "

Ethan said, "Then what?"

Assistant Coach Bob and Ethan jogged around the corner of a building. They came into an open space where Coach Jennifer was hitting golf balls into a deserted pasture.

Assistant Coach Bob stopped jogging and motioned for Ethan to stop. "Run over and talk to Coach Jennifer," he said. "Ask her about the yips."

Ethan wanted to ask why, but Assistant Coach Bob nodded his head and ran off. Ethan walked up to Coach Jennifer. He said, "Hi, Coach. Assistant Coach Bob told me to ask you about the yips."

Jennifer whacked a ball deep into the pasture. She stared into the distance. "The yips," she said, "are flat out dangerous."

"You had them, too?" asked Ethan.

"I used to be a great golfer. Once in a tournament when I was in college, I sliced a ball out of bounds. I'd done it before, but it was extra embarassing for some reason. I finished with a bad round. My next round wasn't any better. Neither was the one after that."

Ethan had never heard Coach Jennifer talk so much. "So what happened?" he asked.

"I finally quit golfing," said Coach Jennifer. "I'm not proud, but I haven't played a tournament in years."

"What?" said Ethan. He was surprised. So much of coaching seemed to be advice on not giving up.

Coach Jennifer put her club into her bag. She said, "It can happen to anyone, even the pros. This one Major Leaguer named Chuck Knoblauch used to play second base. One day he forgot how to throw. He knew how. He just couldn't. They tried moving him to the outfield, but he couldn't throw out there either. He didn't last long after that."

Ethan looked at Coach Jennifer's golf bag. The clubs were worn. The bag was old.

"You need to know what you're up against," said Coach Jennifer. "You can catch the ball. Just work on your blocking until things come around."

Ethan said, "I want to hit the dummy right now."

Coach Jennifer hoisted her golf bag onto her shoulder. "Oh, and one more thing. You need to work on being a better teammate."

Ethan frowned. "Am I a bad teammate?" he asked.

"You could be a little better," said Coach Jennifer. "The Locomotives are about all the players." She laughed. "The Locomotives are even about Assistant Coach Bob and me. Try to enjoy the success of others. Be there to console the failures."

"So what you're saying is I'm too focused on myself?" asked Ethan.

"Yeah," said Assistant Coach Bob. "True team leaders always look for ways to prop up their teammates."

Ethan hadn't thought of himself as self-centered. It bothered him. "Okay," he said. "Thanks for the advice."

Coach Jennifer gave him a big fist bump.

THE BLOCKING DUMMY

At practice the next day, Ethan lined up across from a blocking dummy. When the whistle blew, he smashed his shoulder into the dummy. He kept his arm in close, drove with his legs, and pushed. The dummy moved back six yards.

Ethan lined up again. The whistle blew. He nailed the dummy this time with the palms of his hands. He shoved and drove with his legs.

The players changed stations.

Ethan got into an athletic stance. He heard the whistle and shuffled his feet. He moved sideways. Another whistle meant he was to roll on the ground and spring back up. He kept moving sideways. When the whistle sounded again, Ethan repeated the process. He rolled, sprang back up, and laid his shoulder into a blocking dummy.

At another station, the offense lined up against the defense. Christian was on the offensive side of the ball. He growled at the defensive tackle.

Gavin barked out some signals. "Locomotives ninety-nine! Locomotives ninety-nine! Hut! Hut!"

Gavin tossed the ball to the running back. The play came to Ethan's side. He sealed off the defensive back, and the ball carrier cut up the field.

Coach Jennifer clapped her hands. "Way to seal him off, Ethan. That's how you do it!"

Assistant Coach Bob nodded his head and gave Ethan a thumbs-up.

***

Ethan came in the door of his house. He wasn't surprised to find Dad sitting on the couch and messing around with his phone.

Dad looked up. "Have you been practicing positive visualization?"

"Yep," said Ethan. "I'm all over it."

"Well," said Dad, "you should see what's in the yard. Check it out."

Ethan went out back to the yard. When he flipped on the lights, he saw a new blocking dummy in the middle of the yard. Ethan hustled over to inspect it. It was like the dummies the team used. Ethan gave it a shove and pushed it back a few yards.

He heard Dad yell, "Hey!"

Ethan turned around, and Dad threw him a football. Ethan caught it with one hand.

"Good," Dad said. "You can still catch the ball."

***

The Humboldt Locomotives needed to stay in the race for the conference title. On the sideline, they prepared to square off against the Bronson Ironmen. Coach Jennifer got everyone together. She said, "Who's fired up?"

The players yelled, "We're fired up!"

Assistant Coach Bob said, "Who's fired up?"

The players yelled, "We're fired up!"

Both coaches said, "One, two, three . . . "

And the players yelled, "HUMBOLDT!"

The Locomotives' kickoff team took the field. They stuck the Ironmen at their own thirty-seven. Christian growled as he hustled onto the field with the Locomotive defense.

He stuffed a run on first down, hurried a pass on second, and knocked the ball out of the runner's hands on third. The Ironmen recovered the fumble and punted on fourth down.

Now it was the Locomotives offense's turn. Coach Jennifer called Ethan's number. Ethan really wanted to lay his shoulder into a defender. Instead, he needed to run a slant route. The play called for Gavin to hit Ethan over the middle. Ethan made his usual check with the official at the line of scrimmage.

Gavin put on his act. "Locomotives fifty-five. Humboldt fifty-five. Locomotives. Hut!"

The defensive back was playing ten yards off the line of scrimmage. Ethan took one quick step and slanted to the inside. Gavin gunned the ball.

The linebacker couldn't get in the way to disrupt the pass. Ethan hauled it in and ran for a first down before the safety pulled him down.

A growling Christian came up and smacked Ethan on the shoulder pads. The guys fist-bumped in the huddle.

Coach Jennifer called a lot of running plays after that. The runs gave Ethan the opportunity to lay some blocks on people.

To block the linebackers, Ethan smashed with his shoulders. To block the defensive backs, Ethan kept his arms close to his body and shoved. To block the safeties, he did a combination of both. Ethan thought the blocking felt great.

With the defensive backs playing ten yards off the line, Coach Jennifer ordered up some slants and quick outs to Kenny and Jason.

The Locomotives offense marched down the field. They got inside the twenty.

The Ironmen adjusted. They moved their d-backs closer to the line. Ethan thought a hitch-and-go would be ideal, but then he thought about the drops. Maybe some running plays would be better.

Gavin faked a hand-off to the running back and bootlegged around the end. He came into Ethan's area. Ethan sealed off the defender with a big block.

Gavin took the ball in for a touchdown. After tossing the ball to the referee, Gavin sprinted back to Ethan and slapped him on the shoulder pads.

"Nice block!" Gavin said. "Nice block!"

Ethan could hear Christian before he could see him. Once he saw him, it was too late. Christian picked Ethan up and bear-hugged him. He growled and said, "Nice block!"

The block felt amazing. As Ethan ran to the sideline, he saw Assistant Coach Bob clapping his hands, and Ethan remembered why the block felt so good. He was trying to concentrate on another aspect of his game.

He had caught six passes and not dropped any, but he thought he still had the drops. The team hadn't run a hitch-and-go even though they had been in position to do so.

Ethan wondered if Coach Jennifer would call one later in the game.

She didn't. The Locomotives won with a power running game. Ethan blocked like crazy, but deep down, he was a little disappointed. A successful catch on the hitch-and-go would've felt great.

A win was a win. He was happy enough for the team. He wished, though, he could bring himself to be happier than he was and to show it better. But he was really hoping to prove to himself and his team that he could catch the hitch-and-go.

It was hard for Ethan to accept that Coach Jennifer didn't have enough confidence in him to call the play.

GROWL AND SWAGGER

Ethan couldn't sleep. He just kept tossing and turning in bed. Finally, he turned on his tablet computer and brought up a football video game.

Ethan started on offense. He threw a deep bomb. Complete. He threw another deep bomb. Complete. He threw another deep bomb. Complete.

Before calling the next play, Ethan shut his eyes for a while and relaxed.

***

At school, Ethan ran into Christian in the hallway. Christian growled. They walked to class together.

Christian said, "Dude, you ought to be a lineman, the way you block."

Ethan couldn't tell if Christian was joking or serious. Actually, Ethan wouldn't have minded being a lineman, but he was a bit too skinny. Plus, he enjoyed catching the ball. Other than tight ends, linemen were not allowed to catch the ball. It was against the rules.

"I don't want to play next to you," Ethan said. "You scare me."

"Man up," said Christian. "I scare everyone. You're a good blocker. If you can't catch the ball, you might as well block."

"I can catch the ball," Ethan said.

"Oh, you can?" said Christian.

Ethan asked, "What's that supposed to mean?"

"Nothing," said Christian. "I think you're a good blocker. That's all."

"A good blocker," said Ethan. "Not a good receiver?"

"I didn't say that," said Christian.

"You pretty much did," said Ethan.

Christian put his hand on Ethan's shoulder. He said, "I think you've got a few problems."

Ethan swiped Christian's hand off his shoulder. He asked, "What's *your* problem?"

"I don't have a problem," said Christian. "I think you just need to work on your problems."

"Is it the dropped passes?" asked Ethan.

"Partly," said Christian.

"I'm not talking about last game," said Ethan. "We hardly threw any passes last game."

Christian said, "I wonder why."

Ethan glared and said, "I got this."

"You got what?" asked Christian.

"The deep ball," said Ethan.

"It's more than that," said Christian. "You're selfish."

"What?" said Ethan.

"You never congratulate anyone," said Christian. "If someone else does well, you just get mad that it wasn't you."

"That's not true," said Ethan.

Christian growled. He turned his big shoulders away and went into a classroom.

***

At practice after school, as the players got warmed up, Assistant Coach Bob found Ethan doing some stretches and asked how he was feeling.

"I'm good," said Ethan.

"Good," said Assistant Coach Bob. "You've been blocking like a maniac."

"Yeah," said Ethan. "Christian thinks I should play on the line."

"What's that supposed mean?"

"He thinks I'm a lousy teammate," said Ethan.

"Want me to talk to him?" the coach asked.

"No," said Ethan. "It's fine."

"I think you're doing what you need to do," said Assistant Coach Bob. "Keep blocking. The deep plays will come."

***

When Ethan got home, he felt like playing catch with Dad. But he found Dad pushing around a vacuum cleaner with one hand and tapping away on his phone with the other. Ethan figured he would just let him finish.

Instead of playing catch with Dad, Ethan decided to throw his football up on the roof of the house and catch it as it came down. It was something he used to do as a younger kid. He headed out to the garage to grab a ball. Dad's golf clubs sat in the corner.

The golf clubs made him think of Coach Jennifer. Suddenly Ethan grew terrified. What if he could never get rid of the drops?

What if he ended up like Coach Jennifer and had to quit playing the game he loved?

Ethan hated to admit it, but maybe Dad was right. Maybe Ethan needed some positive visualization. He grabbed his ball and went outside.

Ethan pretended he was playing a game against the Shady Oak Raiders. Instead of playing wide receiver, Ethan was playing all the positions. He stepped up under center, which was weird because the center was also Ethan.

He called out something Gavin would say. "Locomotives eight-nine! Humboldt! Locomotives! Hut, hut!"

He snapped the ball to himself and dropped back. In his head, he ran a deep post pattern. Ethan heaved the ball up on his roof. He watched it come down. He imagined the ball spiraling through the air.

Then as it came down off the roof of his house, he jumped up and grabbed it.

Complete!

In his mind, he ran in for a touchdown. The other Humboldt Locomotives were all Ethans. They ran up and smacked him on the shoulder pads. He smacked them back. It felt great. One of the Ethans even growled at him like Christian.

Enough celebration.

He gathered his team of selves in the huddle. This time, he called the hitch-and-go. They clapped their hands and hustled to the line.

Ethan barked out signals. "Locomotives twelve. Locomotives twelve. Humboldt! Humboldt! Humboldt!"

He dropped back to pass.

He saw himself cut back on the hitch route. He pump-faked. The defender bit on the fake. Ethan the wide receiver turned upfield.

The real Ethan chucked the ball up on the roof. As it came down, Ethan pictured a tight spiral as he sprinted across the hash marks. He saw the ball in the air, looked the ball into his hands, made sure he had control, and ran in for a touchdown.

The other Ethans gathered in the end zone and picked him up. They carried him off the field. On the sideline, they dumped Gatorade over his head.

When Ethan went back inside, Dad had finished vacuuming. He was just shaking his head and staring at his phone. He asked, "Were you doing some positive visualization?"

Ethan shrugged and rolled his eyes. "Yes."

"You were really dialed in," said Dad. "It helps, doesn't it?"

Ethan didn't want to admit that it did. Instead, he went into his room and pretended his clothes were soaked in Gatorade.

CHAPTER 8

DODGE BALL

Once every season, Coach Jennifer took her team of Locomotives to Maximum Dodge Ball. The players, coaches, and parents would hurl dodge balls at each other and then go eat pizza.

On the dodge ball court, Dad ran for his life. Dad's team was down to just Dad. Everyone else had been eliminated.

Ethan's team was down to just Gavin and Ethan. Gavin ran up to the line and hurled the ball.

Dad tried to duck but got nailed on the head.
Game over. Ethan and Gavin had a pretty good laugh.
After Dad recovered, so did he.

As the guys exited their court, Ethan heard
Christian growl from the next court over. He sounded
like an angry bear.

Ethan said to Gavin, "I think that Christian takes
this game too seriously."

Gavin nodded.

Through the netted wall on one of the courts,
Ethan saw Christian hurl a ball at a lineman's head.
The ball smacked off the kid's ear—he was out.
Now both dodge ball teams were down to one player.
It was Christian against the punter.

The punter grabbed the ball and ran up to the line.
He fired it at Christian's knees. Christian jumped over
the throw, retrieved the ball, and moved in on the
punter. The punter retreated.

Christian growled. He reared back, took two
mighty steps, and heaved the ball at the punter's chest.

The punter tried to make the catch, but the ball smacked off his chest, ricocheted into his face, and flew up in the air about ten feet. The punter stumbled backward. The ball landed.

Christian won. He looked toward the waiting area and growled at everyone who had watched his victory.

Ethan said to Dad, "I bet Christian thinks he can go pro in dodge ball."

"Yeah," said Dad. "So does QB3000."

"Maybe they're the same person," said Ethan.

"They could be," said Dad. "You know, we've never seen QB3000."

"We're up," Gavin said to Ethan.

Ethan asked, "Against Christian's team?

"Yes," Gavin said, "against Christian's team."

Ethan high-fived Dad. Then Ethan and Gavin gathered with Mason and Matt, the other guys on their team. Mason played linebacker for the Locomotives. Matt played safety. They agreed their odds of winning would be best if they both went after Christian first.

Gavin started with the ball. He walked up to the line. Most of the other team was lined up near the back out-of-bounds line. Christian stood in front of the other guys. He had his hands on his hips and a big smile on his face. Gavin chucked the ball at Christian's feet.

Christian backed up and fielded the ball off the hop. He growled and charged toward Gavin. Then, right as Christian came up to the line, he changed direction. He reared back and pitched the ball at Ethan's head.

Ethan saw it coming. He positioned his hands to catch the ball but at the last second slid out of the way. He was afraid he would have dropped it.

Christian growled. "I told you," he said. "You can block better than you can catch."

Mason grabbed the ball and flung it at Christian's knees. Christian moved his leg out of the way, but the ball hit one of his teammates to knock him out.

Ethan high-fived Mason for getting an out.

"Right," Christian said to Ethan. "*Now* you congratulate him. Too bad we never see that on the football field."

Ethan and Mason couldn't celebrate for long. One of their opponents had chased down the ball and was rushing toward the line. He fired the ball at Ethan. Ethan took a step backward but caught the ball for an out.

"Ethan caught the ball!" said Christian. "Wow!"

Ethan was upset at Christian's mocking tone. He charged toward Christian but then changed directions to fake him. He hurled a rocket at Christian's remaining teammate and got him out. Now it was three-on-one: Mason, Gavin, and Ethan against Christian. All the balls were on Christian's side, though.

Christian growled. "This is how I like it," he said. "Plenty of ammo. Plenty of room to move." He walked over and picked up two balls. He stood with it and took a deep breath. Then he growled and charged toward the line.

Ethan prepared to catch a bullet, but Christian threw high over his head. He threw the other ball at Mason. The ball nailed Mason in the chest and bounced back over on Christian's side of the court.

Mason was out.

Christian and Ethan retrieved balls.

"The two hot shots on the team," said Christian. "The quarterback and his main target." Christian paused for effect. "One for the money," he said. "Two for show. Three to get ready, and four to . . . " Christian wound up, yelled, "Go!" and threw the ball at Ethan.

The ball came in fast but off-target. Ethan stepped out of the way and watched as Gavin chased down the ball. Gavin, in turn, sprinted at Christian and fired the ball at his head.

Christian ducked the throw, went and grabbed the ball, and charged at Gavin.

Ethan got ready. He figured Christian would fake at Gavin and throw at him.

But Christian didn't fake—he threw the ball at Gavin. When Gavin tried to catch it between his arms and chest, the ball bounced out of his grasp and rolled over near Ethan.

Now it was down to Christian and Ethan. Ethan held the ball.

Christian retreated to the middle of his side of the court. He didn't grab a ball. He just waited. "Let's see who has better hands," Christian said. "Is it the receiver or the lineman?"

Ethan took a few steps to build momentum. He gunned the ball at Christian. The throw went off to the side.

Christian growled running down the ball. He growled as he charged the line. He growled as he threw.

Ethan saw the ball coming right at his chest. He stuck out his hands to catch it, and . . .

He dropped it.

Ethan was out.

Walking off the court, he saw Dad hanging out in the waiting area.

Dad broke into a big smile. "You want to go home and hit the dummy?" he asked.

WHO'S FIRED UP?

Three teams stood at the top of the conference standings. One was the Humboldt Locomotives. Two others each had one loss: the Eagle Bay Eagles and the North Hampton Steelers.

The Locomotives were set to square off against the Eagles. The game was at the Locomotives' home field.

On the sidelines, Coach Jennifer got everyone together. She said, "Big game today!"

Assistant Coach Bob chimed in. He pumped his fist in the air. "If we win," he said, "it'll be us and the Steelers with one loss."

Christian growled.

"If we win," said Coach Jennifer, "we'll stay tied with the Steelers."

Gavin clapped his hands and pumped his fist in the air.

"With a win, we can control our own destiny," said Coach Jennifer. "In sports, you want to control your own destiny."

Ethan wished he could control his own destiny. He was ready to play ball, but in the back of his mind, he wondered if he would drop a pass.

Assistant Coach Bob said, "We just need to take one step at a time."

"We need to get focused, Locomotives," Coach Jennifer said. "Take a few moments. Close your eyes. Picture exactly what you need to do to get your job done."

Ethan shut his eyes. He smiled. Coach Jennifer wanted them to do some positive visualization. He wondered if his dad had put her up to this.

Ethan pictured himself running the hitch-and-go. He broke off the line of scrimmage, cut back, looked for the pump-fake, and ran upfield. Gavin launched a spiral right into his hands . . . complete!

"Open your eyes," said Coach Jennifer. "Now, who's fired up?"

The players yelled, "We're fired up!"

"Everyone get in here," said Coach Jennifer.

The Locomotives gathered around.

They started bobbing, and Coach Jennifer and Assistant Coach Bob clapped and shouted and did their thing. Soon the whole team was jumping up and down on the sidelines.

The Locomotives kicked off, and the Eagles started with the ball. Christian made sure that the Eagles' first possession went nowhere. The Eagles punted, and the Locomotives ended up with decent field position.

Ethan snapped his chinstrap and got ready to take the field. Before he ran out, Assistant Coach Bob found him. "We think we can run the ball on them," he said. "So get ready to lay your shoulder into some guys."

Ethan nodded and hustled out to join his teammates in the offensive huddle.

Coach Jennifer called a run.

On the snap, Ethan shoved the defensive back out of the way. He could feel the run coming his direction, so he cut inside and plowed his shoulder into the linebacker.

The runner followed Ethan's block and wiggled through for a first down. Ethan made a point to congratulate the runner.

Gavin found Ethan as the chains moved. Gavin said, "Nice block, man!"

Ethan waited for Christian to growl at him, but Christian just huddled up and didn't say anything at all.

Coach Jennifer called a flag pattern for Ethan.

Ethan made his check with the official. Gavin went through some signals and received the snap. The linemen went into motion.

The defender played Ethan tightly. Ethan sprinted for six yards, slanted to the inside for three steps, and then cut toward the pylon of the end zone. Ethan had the defender beat by two steps, but Gavin could not get him the ball.

Gavin was running for his life. Two Eagle linemen had chased him out of the pocket. He galloped around the end and dashed past the line of scrimmage. Ethan quit the pattern. He hustled back toward Gavin.

One of the defenders chasing Gavin was the defensive back who had been guarding Ethan. He was closing in when Gavin cut to the side and headed toward Ethan. Ethan shoved the defensive back in the chest and pushed him into the two linemen who had flushed Gavin out of the pocket.

The defensive back and one of the linemen fell down. The other lineman stumbled.

Gavin was free. He ran in for the touchdown. The Locomotives joined him in the end zone and celebrated the score.

Gavin thumped Ethan on the helmet. "Three guys on one play? Dude!"

Ethan thumped Gavin back.

Christian came charging into the celebration. He growled. He hit Ethan on the shoulder pads. He said, "I told you you can block better than you can catch."

On the sideline, Assistant Coach Bob slapped Ethan on the back. "Three guys! One play! Wow!"

"That's how you block, Locomotives," said Coach Jennifer. "That's how you block!"

The Locomotives were denied the two-point conversion but won the game, 6-0. The Eagles defense gave Gavin fits all day, but Humboldt remained at the top of the conference.

They controlled their own destiny.

DESTINY

Ethan woke up early. He still had a few hours before school. He put on some gear and went out to the blocking dummy. Ethan got into an athletic stance and imagined a whistle blowing. He drove his shoulder into the dummy.

The grass had some dew on it. It felt cool on his shoes, but Ethan wanted to roll around in it. He gave himself space. In his head, a whistle blew.

He shuffled his feet and moved sideways. He rolled on the ground and sprang up. Then Ethan came unhinged. He smashed into the dummy and drove it back.

Inside, after his workout, Ethan found Dad making fried potatoes with bacon and eggs. "Want some?" Dad asked. "I added my secret ingredient. It's positive visualization, in case you're wondering."

"I can't get enough of that," Ethan said. "Load me up."

"How many guys will you block next week?" Dad asked, "Maybe four?"

"Eleven," said Ethan. "Plus, I'll catch about eight touchdowns. All bombs on the hitch-and-go."

"That sounds nice," said Dad. "That's the positive visualization talking."

***

That week, every time Ethan ran into Christian in the hallways, the big lineman growled at him.

Christian didn't say any actual words. He just growled and walked off down the hall.

At practice, Ethan pummeled the blocking dummies. At home, Ethan did more of the same.

***

Finally, it was game time.

The Humboldt Locomotives at the North Hampton Steelers. The Locomotives and Steelers remained at the top of the conference. The winner would take the lead.

Coach Jennifer and Assistant Coach Bob rounded up their players. Coach Jennifer said, "Guys, this is why you play the game."

Some guys smacked each other on the pads.

"If we win," Coach Jennifer said, "we control our own destiny."

Christian growled.

"Like last time," said Coach Jennifer, "take a minute and picture what you need to do."

Ethan imagined blocking and short routes. He imagined the hitch-and-go. He broke off the line and cut back. Gavin pump-faked. Ethan accelerated up the field, and Gavin fired a strike. Ethan pulled in the ball and ran for a touchdown.

"All right," said Coach Jennifer. "Who's fired up?"

The players yelled, "We're fired up!"

Assistant Coach Bob said, "Who's fired up?"

The players yelled, "We're fired up!"

Both coaches said, "One, two, three . . . "

And the players yelled, "HUMBOLDT!"

Ethan waited to take the field. Assistant Coach Bob found him. Bob put his arm on Ethan's shoulder pads. "We want to throw the ball," he said. "Be ready."

The Locomotives kick receiving team took the field. They got called for holding on the return and took possession inside their own twenty.

Coach Jennifer called Ethan's number. A slant. Ethan split out wide and motioned to the official to check his positioning. The official nodded.

Gavin barked some signals. "Locomotives one-five. Locomotives one-five. Hut, hut!"

The defensive back bumped Ethan as he came off the line, but Ethan slanted to the inside and ran past him. Gavin threw the ball. Ethan caught it and snuck between the linebacker and safety for a first down.

The running back gained four yards on first down and another four on second down. The Locomotives faced a third and two. Coach Jennifer called a hitch pattern for Ethan.

The center snapped the ball. Ethan charged off the line of scrimmage and broke off his route. Gavin drilled the ball into Ethan's jersey numbers. The defender smacked him right away, but Ethan shook loose and barreled ahead for another first down.

Christian growled at Gavin. He slapped him on the back as the Locomotives huddled, ignoring Ethan.

The Locomotives mixed in some runs with some short passes to the other receivers, Kenny and Jason. They had the ball on the Steelers thirty-four.

Coach Jennifer called a hitch-and go.

Ethan checked with the official to make sure he was on the line. He was. He pictured himself bringing in the ball for a touchdown. He was so focused that he didn't even catch the fake signals Gavin called. All Ethan heard was, "Hut, hut!"

The defensive back was lined up to the inside. He knocked Ethan to the outside. Ethan couldn't get back on his route, so he kept going to the outside. Gavin fired him the ball. Ethan caught it.

He was mad for getting knocked off his route. He secured the ball and shoved the defender with his other hand. The shove was just like delivering a hard block. It threw the defender back. Ethan turned upfield and sprinted in for a touchdown.

All the players congratulated Ethan in the end zone, Christian included. He ran to the sidelines. Assistant Coach Bob smiled and clapped.

Ethan shook his head. "It wasn't a hitch-and-go," he said.

Bob smacked him on the shoulder pads anyway.

Coach Jennifer said, "Nice grab!"

"Yeah," Ethan said, "but I need a hitch-and-go."

As Ethan stood on the sidelines and watched the defense, he got mad at himself. *Did I let the defender push me off the route on purpose?* he wondered. *Maybe I did. If so, what a stupid thing to do! What's my problem? If I can't stand to run the route, I'll never overcome my fear of it.*

Ethan concentrated harder. He thought about running the hitch-and-go to perfection. He concentrated and concentrated and concentrated. Could he control his own destiny?

The Locomotives went in at halftime ahead by a score of 24-16. Ethan could hardly pay attention to the halftime talk. All he could think about was running the hitch-and-go.

The North Hampton Steelers tied the game on the second half kickoff. Their returner burned through the coverage team and went ninety yards for the score.

The Locomotives countered with a controlled running game and short passing attack. Ethan pounded his shoulder into the linebackers and safeties. He shoved defensive backs out of the way. He cleared space for the ball carrier.

After three quarters, the Locomotives were up, 40-32. Both teams were having trouble stopping each other.

Ethan kept waiting for another chance to run the hitch-and-go. He pictured himself catching the ball and going in for a touchdown.

In the fourth quarter, the Humboldt Locomotives got a bit tired. Ethan stood on the sidelines and pictured himself catching the hitch-and-go. The defense gave up big play after big play, and the Locomotives lost their lead.

The Steelers were a big team, and their size seemed to be wearing the Locomotives down. With five minutes to play, Humboldt trailed by six. The offense got the ball on the their own thirty-three.

With the game on the line, Gavin barked out his fake signals. "Humboldt! Humboldt! Hut, hut!"

The defensive backs kept lining up on the inside, but Ethan got open on some out-routes. He shoved tacklers out of the way. The team moved the chains. With under a minute to go, Humboldt lined up for a third and one from the Steelers' eleven. Ethan wanted the ball, but the play call was a quarterback bootleg around the end.

Gavin faked to the running back and sprinted around the end. Ethan had the defensive back shoved to the inside. Gavin kicked it into high gear and broke the plane of the end zone before getting nailed by a safety.

The game was now tied. The Locomotives needed the two-point conversion to take the lead.

Ethan's teammates celebrated. Ethan heard Christian growling, but Ethan had his eyes closed. He was still picturing catching the ball. He was picturing the perfect hitch-and-go.

On the two-point attempt, the running back bulled into the end zone, but Christian got called for holding. The penalty backed them up to the 13-yard line.

Coach Jennifer called time out and talked to the players on the field. "The penalty doesn't hurt us," she said. "It helps us. It gives us more space. We're running the hitch-and-go."

Ethan started breathing heavily. He closed his eyes and imagined catching the ball. Christian growled and smacked him on the shoulder pads. When Ethan opened his eyes, he saw Gavin nodding and smiling at him.

The team broke the huddle. Ethan hustled out wide and motioned to the official to see if he was on the line of scrimmage. The ref nodded.

Gavin went up under center. Gavin was smiling. Ethan could see his grin even behind Gavin's mouthguard. The signals: "Locomotive one-nine. Locomotive one-nine. Hut, hut!"

Ethan sprinted off the line of scrimmage.

The defender cheated to the inside and tried to knock Ethan to the outside. Ethan fought through the initial shoving.

After seven yards, he stopped, cut back, and looked for the ball. Gavin sold the pump-fake. The defensive back, thinking the ball was coming, crashed into Ethan. The ref threw a flag, and Ethan busted up the field.

Gavin tossed the ball over the defense. Ethan saw the perfect spiral coming his way. He looked the ball into his hands. He felt it in the sticky palms of his wide receiver gloves. He pulled the ball tightly against his body and fell down in the end zone.

He had it. The two-point conversion was good. The official raised his arms to signal the score. The Locomotives all piled up on Ethan in the end zone.

Christian growled. "Nice catch," he said. "Nice grab, man!"

As the players unpiled, Gavin hugged Ethan. He bumped him hard right on the facemask to celebrate.

The ref announced that defensive pass interference had occurred on the play. Coach Jennifer, of course, declined the penalty.

Assistant Coach Bob ran onto the field. He hugged Ethan. "You're cured," he said. "You've beaten the yips! I knew you would! You did it, man! You really did it! Great play."

Coach Jennifer ran onto the field. She found Ethan. "I knew you would catch it," she said. "You're going to be fine."

They fist-bumped.

Ethan turned toward the stands. He saw Dad up there nodding. Ethan pumped his fist toward Dad, and Dad pumped his fist back. Then . . .

Ethan's entire uniform was soaked. Gavin and Christian had poured Gatorade over his head.

The Humboldt Locomotives controlled their own destiny. So did Ethan.

ABOUT the AUTHOR

Derek Tellier is the author of *Anderson's Heat, Tae Kwon Do Clash, Wild Receiver,* and *Soccer Sloth.* Growing up in Iowa, he played wide receiver for his high school football team, the Humboldt Wildcats. He currently lives in the Twin Cities where he works as a college professor, writer, and musician.

GLOSSARY

bootleg (BOOT-leg)—a football play in which the quarterback fakes a handoff, hides the ball against his hip, and rolls out

conversion (kuhn-VUHR-zhuhn)—a successful attempt for a point or points especially after a touchdown

hitch-and-go (HICH-AND-GOH)—a pass route run by a receiver in which the receiver begins the route as if running a short pattern where the player stops and looks back as if to catch the pass and then takes off down the field for a longer pattern

huddle (HUD-uhl)—brief gathering of players away from the line of scrimmage to receive instructions, usually from the quarterback, for the next down

line of scrimmage (LINE UHV SKRIM-ij)—an imaginary line in football parallel to the goal lines and tangent to the nose of the ball laid on the ground that marks the position of the ball at the start of each down

out route (OUT ROUT)—a pass pattern where the receiver runs toward the closest sideline

pocket (POK-it)—an area formed by blockers from which a football quarterback attempts to pass

pump-fake (PUHMP-FAYK)—a fake in which a player simulates throwing a pass

pylon (PYE-lon)—one of the flexible, orange-colored upright markers positioned on a football field at the corners of the end zone

possession (puh-ZESH-uhn)—control of the ball

shifty (SHIF-tee)—capable of elusive movement

slant (SLANT)—a short pass pattern where the receiver cuts across the quarterback's field of vision

visualization (vi-zhoo-uhl-ih-ZHAY-shun)—formation of mental visual images

wideout (WIDE-out)—alternate term for receiver

DISCUSSION QUESTIONS

1. Have you ever made a mistake and then had a hard time recovering from it? What was your mistake? How did you get over it?

2. Describe a coach, instructor, or someone who has given you good advice.

3. Why do think Christian growls all the time? Do any of your teammates, friends, or siblings have strange habits like Christian's growling?

WRITING PROMPTS

1. Ethan likes to run the hitch-and-go. Write an exciting description of your favorite sports play.

2. Christian thinks Ethan can be a lousy teammate at times. What makes someone a good teammate? Write a list of at least five qualities. Then pick one and write a paragraph about why this quality is so important.

3. Positive visualization is useful for all kinds of goals and situations. Take a moment and positively visualize something in your future. Then write out what you saw in as much detail as possible.

MORE ABOUT
WIDE RECEIVERS

Jerry Rice, Terrell Owens, Larry Fitzgerald, Randy Moss, and Isaac Bruce are the top five leaders in all-time receiving yardage in the National Football League (NFL).

Wide receivers can wear only certain numbers in the NFL. They can have 11–19 and 80–89.

Wide receivers are also called receivers, wideouts, split ends, flankers, or slot backs.

Each NFL team usually carries 3–5 wide receivers on their roster.

In 2002 Marvin Harrison of the Indianapolis Colts set the NFL record for most catches in a season. The favorite target of quarterback Peyton Manning hauled in an amazing 143 receptions.

WIDE RECEIVER PATTERNS

hitch-and-go

10

hitch

20